A NEW LIFE on the MOON

When the boy awoke the next morning, he remembered everything. "On the night of the blue moon, anything can happen," he said to the cat. And sometimes it does.

Soon they saw the lights of home, and
as quick as a wish, they were safe and warm
in their own bed.

"The Earth is blue," said the boy.
"A blue planet."

But as he was thinking how perfect
it would be, he looked out into the
darkness and thought of home.

He shivered, and he tried not
to think of how lonely it was
to be out here in the deep
darkness of space.

The boy looked and looked
and thought he could see the yellow
porch light twinkling, but perhaps
it was just a star.

He took his cat in his arms,
and together they dove into the dark,
down and down, until they could see
the Earth ahead of them.

"We could stay here forever," said the boy.
"We could make a new life on the moon."

They ran and jumped
and tumbled and flew.

The boy collected moon rocks
and skipped them through the air,
counting as they flew: one, two, three . . .
and on and on.

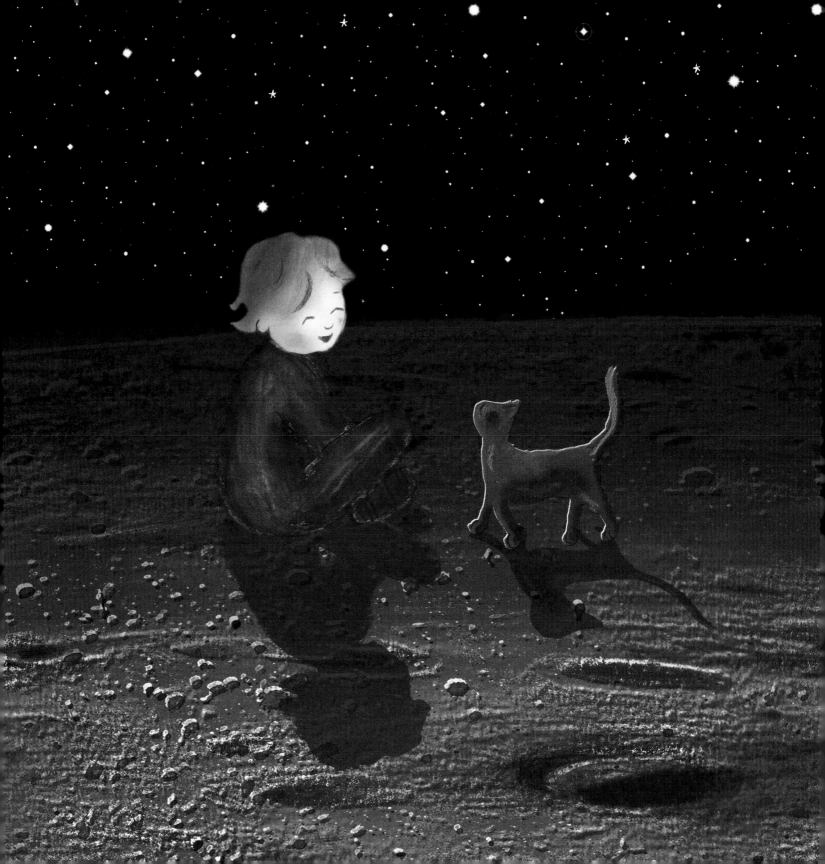

When everything stopped, they were on the moon, which was exactly as the boy had always known it would be:

perfect.

The little boat was suddenly
bathed in a wash of light that
swirled them round and round, and
the boy took his cat in his arms.

Down and down they went,
but somehow the whole time
they were traveling down,
they were also traveling up.

But tonight he wished extra hard.
And the cat wished too.

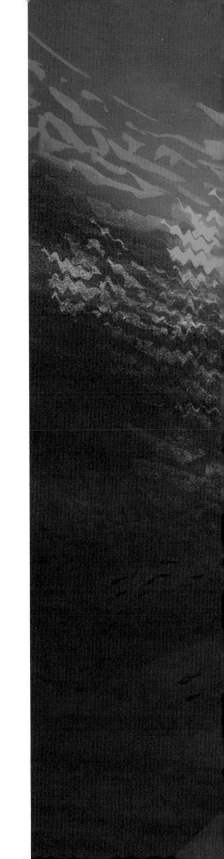

Never had the moon seemed so within his reach.
Wish-wish, said the waves lapping the side of the boat.

As the boy rowed closer and closer, he wished that
he could go to the moon.

This was a wish he'd made many times before.
He'd thought about living on the moon while lying
in his bed and reading his books. He'd gazed out the
window and imagined what that life would be like.

In the middle of the lake was a second moon,
shimmering and shining. The boy steered the
boat toward it.

The cat ran ahead, and the boy
followed. There was a boat at the edge
of the lake, so they jumped right in.

A lake appeared where there'd never been a lake before. It was deep and blue, a very deep, deep blue. The waves made a little lapping sound on the shore that was somehow part of the same song the boy had been hearing since he'd left the house.

The path through the forest was as familiar
to the boy as any room in his house,
but tonight, it was different.

The trees of the forest
were blue as well, and
somewhere high in the branches,
something was singing. It might have
been birds or it might have been dragons.

The cat and his boy walked through the bluebells toward the forest.

A hundred thousand tiny bells were ringing out a song that no one had ever heard before.

"On the night of the blue moon,
anything can happen," said the boy.

On the night of the blue moon, a boy and his cat
went for a walk.
    Inside their house the light was warm and yellow,
but outside it was blue and magical.

THE BOY AND THE
Blue Moon

SARA O'LEARY

illustrated by ASHLEY CROWLEY

GODWINBOOKS

Henry Holt and Company
New York

For Liam, my darling boy
—S. O'L.

For Mom, Dad, and my sister, Sam
—A. C.

Henry Holt and Company, *Publishers since 1866*
Henry Holt® is a registered trademark of Macmillan Publishing Group, LLC
175 Fifth Avenue, New York, New York 10010 • mackids.com

Library of Congress Cataloging-in-Publication Data is available.
ISBN 978-1-62779-774-0

Our books may be purchased in bulk for promotional, educational, or business use.
Please contact your local bookseller or the Macmillan Corporate and Premium Sales Department
at (800) 221-7945 ext. 5442 or by e-mail at MacmillanSpecialMarkets@macmillan.com.

First edition, 2018 / Designed by Patrick Collins
The artist used blue inks applied using a water brush pen, gouache paint, graphite sticks, pastels,
colored pencils, and Adobe Photoshop to create the illustrations for this book.
Printed in China by RR Donnelley Asia Printing Solutions Ltd., Dongguan City, Guangdong Province

1 3 5 7 9 10 8 6 4 2

BLUE MOONS

THE SUPER MOON

THE SUPER MOON